The Lots Were Cast

Nicole Fratrich

Story, typesetting, and design by Nicole Fratrich. Cover images generated using Canva's Magic Media app. Interior images are used under Canva's Content License Agreement.

Typeset in Ancient Kai and Calibri.

ISBN: 979-8-9866111-3-6 (Print)

For all who have guided, inspired, and nurtured my faith...

And for my former Theology students who insisted on calling me

Mother Frat!

"When the soldiers crucified Jesus, they took his clothes, dividing them into four shares, one for each of them, with the undergarment remaining. This garment was seamless, woven in one piece from top to bottom.

'Let's not tear it,' they said to one another. 'Let's decide by lot who will get it.'

This happened that the scripture might be fulfilled that said, 'They divided my clothes among them and cast lots for my garment.'

So this is what the soldiers did."

JOHN 19: 23-24

The head of Emperor Tiberius Caesar flipped in the air and landed

on the ground with a soft thud, kicking up dust.

For a moment the deafening roar of cheering faded, and all he

could focus on was the sunken coin in the dirt.

"Cassius, you've won the last lot of the day!" Cornelius' gravelly voice pulled Cassius back to the crowd where he was standing in a close circle of fellow sweaty Roman soldiers.

Groans of disappointment accompanied a tossed bloody tunic.

Cassius caught it swiftly with one hand and then stared at it. He rolled the garment in his hands, amazed that he now possessed a piece of clothing that belonged to Jesus the Nazorean, the one that had just been crucified up the hill at Golgotha. He could still hear the shouts of rage and sharp wails from the crowd who had followed Jesus to the Place of the Skull.

Cassius tried not to form an opinion as to whether or not the so-called "King of the Jews" deserved this death. As a devoted Roman soldier, it was ingrained in his entire being to remain loyal to his country and obey the commands given to him. He rarely had time to try and rationalize the motives for his duties, as Roman culture demanded progress. Keep moving, keep pushing, and never look back. When he dared to reflect, he always found himself unsure of what to believe. In the end he trusted his leaders. He was sure that Caesar and Pilate had their valid reasons.

Besides, he had just spent all morning pushing people away from the Nazorean. Now close to three o'clock in the afternoon, Cassius was relieved of his duties for the day and headed across the city.

Suddenly a crack of thunder shook the sandy ground beneath him. His heart skipped a few beats, and he heard women's screams echoing around him.

By the time he managed to get his bearings, a wave of more shouting came closer as people stumbled out of their doors in a frenzy.

Then he spotted a fellow soldier.

"Tyquavius, what news?"

Tyquavius skidded to a halt; his sword clenched in his hand. "The Jewish temple," he panted in between heavy gasps. "The sanctuary veil's been torn in two!"

Cassius and Tyquavius fought through the crowd, which included faithful Jews kneeling on the ground, praying rapidly in between tears. Sighing, Cassius decided that he'd had enough of weeping people for the day.

As they stood in front of the temple and heard anxious chatter around them, Cassius realized that the sanctuary veil was as important to the Jewish faith as the temple traditions of his own Roman gods.

Caiaphas, the high priest of that year, followed his father-in-law Annas, who had been the previous Jewish high priest. Their dark robes rustled behind them as they rushed to the temple entrance. Their heads disappeared inside the temple for a while, so Cassius and Tyquavius helped the other soldiers in the area push back the growing crowd.

After nearly fifteen minutes, the high priest and his predecessor emerged, Annas wearing his typical neutral facial expression as he pushed Caiaphas forward. The son-in-law, although not seeming as composed, raised his hand in the air and began to address the people in his deep, bold voice:

"Our mighty and powerful Lord has shaken the earth. Although slow to anger, our Father's wrath, in response to the false teachings of Jesus the Nazorean, has torn the veil that separates the high priests from God Himself, the Holy of Holies where the Ark of the Covenant once resided."

Caiaphas then explained how sacrifices and worship would still be conducted following this tragic occurrence. Before the men exited, Annas slightly pushed Caiaphas aside so he could address his Israelite brothers and sisters. Just a few years ago Annas had been deposed of his prominent position as high priest, but his remaining power and influence meant that his words were still respected.

Annas lifted his head and looked down upon the people. "Children of Israel, you've often heard our beloved sanctuary veil be referred to as the 'tunic of God.' Although our tunic has been torn, remember that we wear a tunic for God every day we have on this earth. We are a chosen people, chosen to do our Lord's will. Now go home and take refuge in our Lord God of Hosts!"

Cassius chuckled to himself as he realized that he had just won a tunic formerly owned by a child of Israel. The crowd began to thin, but as Cassius turned to leave, he heard a Jewish woman nearby whisper to another next to her:

"What if the rumors are true? What if that man was the messiah?"

"Oh, come off it," her friend said, rolling her hazel eyes. "We can't know for sure that the Lord connected the crucifixion this morning with the sanctuary veil. We're not worthy to know these things, Esther. At any rate, that man couldn't have been the chosen one."

The women slowed their pace, but Cassius didn't mind. He was intrigued by the conversation and was glad to linger within earshot as he walked.

"And why not?" Esther demanded. "Haven't you heard about all of those miracles he was said to perform?"

"I heard about them, but I haven't seen them."

"But Sarah, the Nazorean said he would destroy the temple and raise it again in three days! The temple is shattering before our eyes, starting with the veil!"

Sarah's tone grew sharper. "Well perhaps we'll just have to wait three days then to see if the man was a crazed zealot or godly leader."

"And behold, the veil of the temple was torn in two from top to bottom; and the earth shook and the rocks were split. "

MATTHEW 27: 51

Cassius and Tyquavius headed separate ways, allowing Cassius time to reflect. Both women had valid points. Still, it wasn't his place to make a decision one way or another. All he knew was that he had won a heavily blood-stained garment from a man now dead, one who was pierced by nails. Besides, the Jewish God couldn't be more powerful than the Roman deities combined.

Upon sneaking into the chamber room, as not to be seen from the outside corridor, Cassius was greeted by Livy, who ran directly to him.

She immediately tried to throw her arms around him, until he stopped her.

"Don't. I'm covered in blood."

Livy backed away quickly as her high cheekbones blushed in panic. "Not yours?"

"No," he said as he leaned his spear in the corner of the doorway. Gently, he set the crimson-tipped helmet on top of the spear.

"The crucifixion of that Nazorean was brutal. I've never seen so many angry people at a crucifixion before. Between keeping the Jews at bay and helping push the Nazorean along, I honestly can't tell you whose blood it is."

"This Jesus must've done something awful to rile them up like that," Livy said.

"That's just it," Cassius said as he moved towards a basin of water so he could wash himself. "I've seen a prophet crucified before, but this was beyond any rage I've ever seen. There were Jewish people who begged Pilate to have the man killed."

"But was he a criminal?"

"I heard his followers called him Rabbi."

"That doesn't mean he didn't go against the law."

Cassius splashed his grimy face with the cold water. "Livy, I just don't know. But what's done is done. No changing it now." He patted his dripping face with a nearby cloth. "Besides, if—"

"Sh!" Livy shuffled to the chamber door, arms swinging as she went. She leaned toward the doorway and listened.

"Quick! My father's coming."

Livy pushed Cassius away from the basin and behind her trifold dressing screen. "Don't move!"

"I think I can manage." Cassius rolled his eyes and held his breath.

When Livy opened the door, a tangle of robes billowed through the doorway to greet her. She traced the fine embroidery until she met her father's serious gaze. A nobleman with a chin that jutted forward and a sunken face that hid wrinkles well, Aurelius was well-respected and trusted when it came to being a patron for young men enlisting in the Roman military. Without a patron to recommend him to service, a man's military career lay in shambles because it could never get started.

Aurelius happened to be Cassius' patron.

"Livy," Aurelius' voice boomed, "did I not tell you stay away from the city today?"

Livy nodded, her auburn curls bobbling. "Father, I haven't set foot outside today."

"Ah," Aurelius pointed his finger at her now, "but the servants tell me you were watching the Nazorean from the balcony. A young Roman noblewoman should not concern herself with such affairs."

"Father, I wasn't outside very long. I hardly saw anything but a raging crowd. Then I came back inside."

Aurelius turned on his heel, robes whirling with him. "Very well. But don't forget your place. Soon you'll be handed over in marriage to continue our noble bloodline. There's no need to attend to political matters, especially those that refer to the— what did they call him? — King of the Jews."

Once Aurelius departed, satisfied with her daughter's answers, Cassius shuffled out from behind the dressing screen and finally embraced Livy.

"We can never tell him." She buried her head in his broad shoulder.

"He doesn't have to know."

"But he'll arrange a husband, and then there will be no hope for us."

"Maybe we'll run away."

"He'd kill us both."

"Let him try. We'll be quicker."

"Pilate's added me to the change of guard for the Nazorean's tomb!" Tyquavius spoke quickly.

"Sounds incredibly boring—to watch over the dead," Cassius answered.

"Could be interesting if the prophet's disciples flock back."

"They had him killed, so why come back?"

Tyquavius shrugged. "His friends could try to steal his body. You never know."

Three days after Tyquavius was assigned as a tomb guard, Cassius met a stranger in the shell of the friend he used to know.

Early that morning, just at the rise of dawn, Tyquavius and Marcus busted through a side corridor of Pilate's palace and made their way to Cassius.

"Quick!" Marcus said, panting, we must speak with the governor."

"At this hour?" Cassius folded his arms. He glanced over at Tyquavius and noticed the fearful glimmer in his eyes. This matter must be serious if someone jovial like Tyquavius looked frightened to death.

"What's this about? Cassius continued his interrogation.

Tyquavius murmured, "The tomb...it's empty."

Cassius' face twitched as he processed the information. "It's what?"

"It—"

"It's empty," Marcus agreed. "Jesus is not there."

"Maybe this isn't a Roman problem," Cassius suggested. "We need to consult Annas and Caiaphas."

"And not report to Pilate?" Marcus struggled to keep his voice to a hush.

"You know that Caiaphas and the governor work together to negotiate between Romans and Jews. Leave this task to the high priest, not us."

Both Caiaphas and Annas went silent upon hearing the news. Annas sat down slowly and rested his head on his fist. Caiaphas stared at the floor, not lifting his eyes, even when Cassius succumbed to a dry, dust-induced cough.

After the two men had time to digest the situation and discuss with each other, Caiaphas stepped forward to address the soldiers before him. "You will forget everything you saw, or think you saw. As far as the governor is concerned, tell him that Jesus' disciples stole his body in the night. We will not speak of this event again."

Caiaphas paid the men and then asked them to leave.

" While the women were on their way, some of the guards went into the

city and reported to the chief priests everything that had happened.

When the chief priests had met with the elders and devised a plan, they

gave the soldiers a large sum of money, telling them, 'You are to say,

" His disciples came during the night and stole him away while we were

asleep. "

If this report gets to the governor, we will satisfy him and keep you out

of trouble. ' So the soldiers took the money and did as they were

instructed. And this story has been widely circulated among the Jews to

this very day. "

MATTHEW 28: 11-15

Cassius, having spent the past few years serving Pilate closely,

sensed that the governor was feeling a bit off, even after Caiaphas smoothed things over about Jesus' disappearance. For the most part,

Pilate's stoic facial expression remained the same. He followed the same

everyday routines, and he still offered a pride smile when conducting

business with other elected officials.

Ever since that fatal Friday, when he washed his hands and

completed his civic duty to keep peace among the people, Pilate acted as

though he wasn't bothered by the entire situation. However, Cassius,

from time-to-time, noticed the governor staring off into the distance

more frequently. His appetite wasn't as grand and ravishing, and he

preferred to spend more time in solace or consoling his wife, who had

been having disturbing dreams lately.

So when Pilate announced that he would be hosting a banquet for

his noblemen friends, Cassius was relieved to see his leader being

sociable again. What he hadn't counted on was Pilate's inviting Aurelius'

daughter to the celebratory dinner.

On the night of the banquet, Cassius was given his duties.

"Cassius!" Pilate strode proudly across the room and laid an outstretched hand on Cassius' shoulder. "Tonight will be marvelous. Ever since the death of that Nazorean, this city has been anxious and rattled."

"Sir, I couldn't agree more."

"In any case, I want you to guard the dining quarters tonight. There have been strange tales that the resurrected dead have been roaming town, and I'd prefer no chaos tonight. I've always trusted you, Cassius. You have a firm head on your shoulders."

Livy's dress was an oceanic blue and the hem rested right above her ankles. Her golden hoop earrings dangled each time she shook her head in laughter. Her bronze skin added to her radiance, further proving that she was her father's delight—a true, cultured daughter of a Roman nobleman.

Cassius inhaled a deep breath upon seeing Livy enter Pilate's banquet room with her arm wrapped around her father's. Cassius knew deep down that all the caution he could muster would never allow him to fully be with Livy. Even if her father never discovered their affair, there was no way Cassius could prevent Livy from marrying someone else at her father's request.

As he stood nearby the banquet table, he fiddled with his sword's scabbard, tracing the engraved Roman insignia with his calloused fingers. To love Livy was to also betray his own country. His purpose as soldier was to defend Rome and bring her to fullest glory. He had taken an oath of loyalty to the state. In Rome, married men couldn't serve in the military. He promised honor over romantic attachment.

Of course, he would eventually be given the freedom to select a wife and generate the next population of Roman warriors, but it was considered complete betrayal to lust after your own patron's daughter, not to mention while actively serving the governor! Cassius deeply respected and admired Aurelius. In fact, Aurelius had more compassion than most patrons, but he instilled in Cassius a deep love for country and a willingness to sacrifice one's life for the sake of that country. But loving Livy and treating her with dignity didn't guarantee a father's blessing.

Now Cassius' attention was drawn to the table where Pilate just finished his welcome speech. The attendants began rushing in and out of the room with plates of food as the nobles dined and chatted. Eventually, the dinner conversation turned to the strange occurrences that had taken place since the crucifixion of Jesus.

"Have you heard about the strange reports of the dead rising from the grave?" asked Flavius, a patron whose widened eyes spoke more words than his mouth.

"Come, Flavius," Pilate said. "Don't succumb to such nonsense."

"But Governor, I've seen one myself!"

Snickers and low chortles echoed around the room. Even Livy grinned.

Flavius stood up and stamped his foot, robes wrestling as he did so. "Don't you remember that old Jewish man who died after being trampled by his own livestock? Well, I saw him this morning in the city."

"You must've been out in the sun too long," someone down the table jeered.

"I know what I saw!"

Suddenly the banquet room erupted with shouts and overlapping voices as the nobles began arguing with each other over the presence of resurrected dead and what they should do about it, as well as how to prevent the spread of Jesus' teachings.

At this point, the men were pointing fingers, shaking fists, and waving arms. Besides spitting hot breath at each other, the nobles, in Cassius' opinion, weren't causing any physical altercations that needed broken up. Meanwhile, the noblemen's wives simply observed their husbands, knowing that it wasn't their place to interfere.

It was then that Livy, after rolling her eyes at her father's protesting, gently slipped from her seat and met Cassius in the corner where he was standing guard.

"What are you doing?" he mumbled. "Your father is right there and will spot us! All he has to do is turn his head."

She put a finger to his lips. "Sh. No, he won't."

Livy pulled Cassius through the side archway, squeezing past a servant about to enter the chaotic room with a tray full of golden honey cakes and bittersweet Torta di Ricotta e Visciole with cherries on top. Once the sugary aromas drifted away, she wasted little time in pressing her lips to his.

Cassius couldn't say he fully hated this situation, but he was also completely aware of the dangers involved. At the same time, he could almost vanish in this blissful moment. He practically did so, too, until he heard a sharp clatter, followed by yelling.

"CASSISUS! CASS—LIVY!"

The panicked voice belonged to Aurelius. He instantly used his flabby arms to rip Cassius away from his daughter.

"Dishonorable brute!" He slapped Cassius.

"Father, don't!" Livy screamed.

"I will not tolerate my daughter being disrespected, let only disrespected by a soldier I commended."

"He didn't disrespect me."

Aurelius paused. Then the welled-up anger in his face slowly spread to a shocked confusion. Before he could process what his daughter just said, the governor burst in.

The governor also froze, eyes widened. Once he pieced together the situation, he folded his arms and smirked.

"A man forgets his place, eh Cassius?"

Cassius felt the sweat bead on his forehead while the other nobles from the banquet hall began to inch closer toward the drama, no doubt so they could gossip later.

"I swear to you, Governor," Cassius said, "my loyalty remains."

Pilate lifted his head and scoffed. "Your loyalty to me by your sword? Or your loyalty to your heart?" Then his tone unexpectedly sweetened, and he outstretched his arms. "But now and then a man

must release tension and please a woman."

At first Cassius felt relieved at Pilate's smirk, thinking that he

wouldn't be punished for abandoning his post. But when the smirk

narrowed and slanted, he knew in his gut that he would face the

consequences of his love for Livy.

"Your loyalty to your own patron, though..." the governor broke

off and began pacing, his arms behind his back. "That is punishable by a

variety of means...flogging...stripping of military

honors...torture...banishment from the city..."

Cassius' nerves were churning as Pilate spoke. He needed to think

of a plan quickly, or he and Livy would be parted forever. The only thing

he hadn't counted on was Livy having her own secret plan.

While Pilate continued rambling about possible punishments,

Livy's body suddenly swayed backwards as she fainted into her father's

arms. The nobles crowded around Aurelius, and Pilate even turned to see

what was the matter.

The distraction worked. Cassius made a great escape and charged out the window, clutching onto the drape as he did so. By the time one of the nobles realized Livy's devious feat and a fellow soldier was commanded by Pilate to "sever the curtain no matter how dull your blade," Cassius had climbed down the wall of the palace. The drape was long enough that, when he was only a few feet from the ground, he had ample room to jump safely. Granted, his whole body hit the ground and rolled through dust, but he was out.

Time, however, was not on his side. Livy had "awaken" from her fainting spell and pushed her way through the sweaty nobles and tumbled out the window herself, her father screaming bloody murder all the while.

The only luck Cassius had was that his horse was tied on that side of Pilate's palace. His fingers were numb and shaky as he scrambled to release the knot in the rope. Meanwhile Livy jumped into the saddle and waited for her love.

Cassius felt the reins loosen just as his peer soldiers leaned out the window above and prepared to send down a volley of arrows. He swung his leg over his ebony horse, and Livy instantly wrapped her arms tightly around his waist.

Roman soldiers were bred to be precise. Patrons insisted upon it. The higher ranks demanded it. The governor relied on it. And Pilate got his wish.

The horse had almost vanished around the corner and out of sight when one arrow clipped Livy. Well, that's what Cassius thought. Livy wasn't just grazed by the arrow—it pierced a calf muscle.

Naturally, she shrieked and then clutched onto Cassius even tighter so she wouldn't slip off the horse.

Somehow, by the grace of a god, they escaped the city.

Galilee. That's where he decided to go. Egypt was no place for a Roman, but if he lost himself in some little Galilean town, he could use his soldier's prestige, hopefully before word spread that a soldier had gone rogue and fled.

Rogue? Nothing could be further from the truth! Cassius was proud to serve, and he never intended to violate protocol. All because he became a slave to his heart!

After successfully fleeing the city, Cassius knew he had to stop and tend to Livy's injury before she could safely travel any farther. He finally found a patch of shade trees swaying in the rare wind, and he gently lifted Livy from the horse and onto the ground.

He didn't have anything soft for her to lie on, which made him feel less than manly as she wailed in pain. So much for being a stoic soldier who protects women, he thought to himself.

"Why did you come with me?" he suddenly chastised her.

Livy bit her tongue. "That was our escape. Now we can build our life together."

"You do realize that now there's no going back?"

"We'll figure something out—" her sentence turned into another wail.

Cassius knelt next to her. "We have to pull the arrow out."

The arrow cut deep, no doubt about that. If he didn't succeed on the first try, the pain would worsen due to a shattered arrow tip.

After a shaky breath, he told Livy to clench a nearby tree root to brace herself for the impending pain of an extracted arrow. He wished he had a third hand because he wasn't sure that all his strength would be enough. He was left panting, but he got the arrow out.

"Damn it!" Cassius looked down at the broken tip of the arrow and the swollen gash in his lover's leg. Then, after his delayed reaction, he realized the amount of blood seeping from the wound.

"Cass—" She was fading in and out of consciousness now.

He groped around him frantically, wondering what he could use to make a tourniquet around the wound.

The lot. His gambling reward. It was stuffed in one of his saddlebags. He skidded over to his horse and tore through the bag. Time was precious, so if he had no other choice but to use a dead man's bloodied tunic for a medical emergency—oh well. If it caused an infection in Livy's leg, he'd deal with that later. Truth be told, she'd likely lose the limb thanks to the lodged arrow tip.

Once tightly tied, the garment served its purpose. The blood stopped gushing, but Livy wasn't well, and Cassius couldn't hold a vigil. He was a wanted man. Or was he? Would Pilate consider him a criminal? He'd broken no laws; however, Pilate did like to prove a point, even if that meant public shame.

And then there was Aurelius. He wouldn't abandon his daughter so simply. Yes, Cassius decided. The Roman army, even if just a few soldiers, would be searching for him. Staring at a sleeping Livy, he hesitated before hoisting her onto the saddle in front him so he could hold both her and the reins at the same time.

The horse staggered into Galilee—just barely. It was twilight now, which meant that Cassius would have an easier chance at moving around unnoticed.

He couldn't hold onto Livy anymore. Her skin was so pale and clammy. Cassius was no medical expert, but he was certain she had a fever due to a brewing infection. He knew he couldn't wait too much longer to choose a decent hiding spot, so he chose the first dilapidated barn he came across.

After gently placing Livy on a patch of hay inside the barn, he checked his surroundings. No Jews. No Romans. Perfect.

It was a long night. Cassius nodded off several times, but he spent most of his time peeking outside the barn doors and watching Livy sleep as he caressed her hair. By early morning, as the sun began to rise, he couldn't help but pace. Livy was burning up and he hated to risk going outside of the barn. But he didn't have much of a choice.

Cassius stepped outside into the early morning and was greeted by a thin layer of humid fog. He scanned the houses in front of him, wondering where the town well was located. He turned and headed behind the rows of houses, so not to be noticed.

The farther he walked, the more nervous he became. Where was the well?! It couldn't have been far. He felt the morning heat start to rise, as well as a sinking feeling in the pit of his stomach. He couldn't leave Livy alone much longer, and the Nazoreans would soon be out and about.

Out of nowhere, a soft breeze picked up and nearly gave Cassius goosebumps, drying the sweat on his toned biceps.

"*Sequi* (Follow)."

While whipping his head around to look behind him, Cassius said, "Hello?"

No one in sight.

"*Sequi aqua* (Follow to water)."

Dreamily, Cassius followed the voice. Maybe he had been out in the sun so long lately that his mind was toying with him. But the voice was almost a whisper, and he found it mesmerizing.

When Cassius laid eyes on the cistern, he pinched himself to make sure his imagination hadn't run away with his Roman logic. Had he actually heard a voice? Perhaps the words he thought he had heard weren't really distinguishable. Someone else could have been here talking. But it was still early morning. No one in the Jewish city was up and about yet save for one ruffled Roman soldier desperately seeking water to save his lover.

He pilfered a small bucket from a nearby yard, as petty thievery was the least of Cassius' problems. He swiftly found his way back to the barn and stood frozen in the doorway, a goat braying to announce his arrival. But that wasn't all. A middle-aged Nazorean couple was hovering over Livy's body on the straw.

"Move away from her!" Cassius yelled from behind, causing the woman to jump.

The man instinctively drew a tiny blade, but he dropped it quickly upon realizing Cassius' status.

"Don't hurt her! She's in a critical state."

The couple stepped aside, and Cassius now stared into Livy's dull, but very much alive, eyes."

"Livy!" Cassius slid on his knees to be next to her on the ground.

He fingered her cheek, then her neck, then her chest, in awe that she was conscious and looking much better.

He glanced up at the man. "I am not here to hurt you or your family. I'm only here to help her heal. But tell me, what did you do to make her so well?"

The man played with his beard, shrugged, and said, "Nothing. We did not cure her."

Then the woman lifted a bloody white garment and showed Cassius. "I removed this to check the wound. Look, sir, her leg is healed."

No. This just couldn't be. That was impossible. Livy had been clinging to life just an hour ago. This made no sense at all.

Yet the woman was right. The arrow wound on Livy's leg was sealed and scarred over, as if she had simply tripped and cut herself.

The woman, turning to her husband, said quietly, "the children will be awake soon. I must go back inside."

With his wife gone, the man seemed more confident to speak. "How can I be sure to trust your word?"

Cassius straightened to his feet. "You can't. I'm a Roman soldier who's not fond of Jews. But right now, I need your barn."

"So you are hiding."

"You could say that."

"Then we'll pay the price if you're found."

"I'll see to it that won't happen."

The man scowled in response and prepared to leave.

"Call me Cassius." He figured that friendliness might ease the tension.

"I am Aron."

Cassius chuckled. "A relative of Moses' cousin?"

"No," Aron cracked a grin, "but I'm glad to see you know a bit of Jewish history."

After drinking water from the well, Livy's color began to flourish. Cassius spent most of the day holding and caressing her. Toward evening, she began to hold a conversation. What she said first, however, was neither what Cassius expected nor wanted.

"I'm going back home to my father, alone."

"You're what?"

"It's better that way, for both of us."

For a solid minute he could only gape at her. "What problem does that solve, for either of us?"

"Cassius, you're considered a traitor now. Even if my father and Pilate don't order you to be executed, you'll be banned from the city."

Cassius hung his head and stared at the ground, contemplating as Livy draped her arms around him.

"It's not that I don't love you," she said.

"Then why go back?" he answered sharply.

"I—" she lowered her voice, "the linen that you wrapped around my injured leg—I know where it came from. Cassius, I'm a nobleman's daughter. If word were to get around that I was supposedly healed by clothes worn by that crucified prophet—"

He couldn't believe what he was hearing. Just moments ago, he was thrilled to see her healed, and now his dreams were shattering.

Cassius laughed wryly. "Livy, you just don't tell anyone. Don't be dramatic about this."

Livy's face hardened. "I'm not being dramatic. I'm being pragmatic. I was a fool to think that you and I would have ever have a chance."

Standing up to tower over her, Cassius said, "Afraid of your father, is that it?"

She shrugged. "You know he'll be looking for me, if he's not already."

Cassius sighed. He hated to admit it, but Livy was right. Aurelius was likely scouring nearby cities for word of his precious daughter. Instead of disowning his daughter, he'd drag her back home and take up vengeance with the soldier he helped to train all those years ago. Standing there limply, Cassius was beginning to accept that, no matter how the dice rolled, he was the one who had done a dishonorable act, even if he didn't believe it himself. Rome would be against him.

In the grand scheme of things, Pilate would have graver matters to attend to rather than worry about a Roman soldier who ran off with a patron's daughter. But Aurelius...no, he would never forget.

Cassius' luck was running out.

Once Livy had left by horse to Jerusalem, Cassius made an agreement with Aron to continue lying low in the barn. He had a lot of planning to do.

That evening, near sunset, Cassius sat on a pile of straw and watched the animals eat supper. He wondered what life would be like as an outcast. Without a soldier's rank, who would he be? Who could he be?

Suddenly he heard a low chirp near the barn window, stirring him from his melancholy. Peering out the window, he spotted a myna bird stumbling in his direction. Instead of pecking the ground for food, this bird would stop every few inches after waddling. With its yellow beak, it would poke its left wing.

When the bird finally turned sideways, Cassius noticed the injured wing. The bird had gotten cut, as tiny drops of blood fell from the wing and trailed behind.

Cassius had an idea.

He was so fascinated by the bird and consumed by his idea that

he forgot he was hiding from the outside world. Holding the cloth that

had belonged to Jesus of Nazareth and had healed Livy, Cassius tiptoed

his way outside.

He approached the bird slowly. When its head was turned, Cassius

gently, but swiftly, scooped up the bird into the garment and hurried

back inside the barn.

"Sh-sh-sh," Cassius soothed the bird, who began to squirm inside

the garment. It finally poked its beak through an opening in the tangled

cloth. He continued to hold the garment firmly around the bird,

increasing pressure on the injured wing.

"It's funny," he spoke to his new acquaintance, "that you show up

when my life is in shambles."

Myna birds were considered bad luck in his culture.

"You know, when I brought you in here, you were bleeding pretty

heavily."

As he started to loosen the pressure with which he held the garment, he realized that the bird's blood droplets weren't visible on the cloth. In fact, the garment wasn't even wet. The reddish-brown stains of dried blood were the same as when Cassius won the lot. He hadn't even paid attention to Livy's blood, but apparently this garment had no recollection of her wound either. Carefully, he unwrapped the bird, who had stopped chirping incessantly. Cassius grinned slightly. He was right. The bird flapped its wings as if it were never injured. No visible cut or impaired wingspan. It was healed.

Giddy at this discovery, Cassius just had to try one more experiment. Quickly, he drew a small blade that he carried and, with barely a wince, made a slice on his forearm. Then, gathering the garment, he wrapped it tightly around the cut. He closed his eyes and focused on the cut's sting and the throbbing pulse. With his eyes closed, he waited five minutes. By then his forearm hardly hurt. He tore the garment off and just gaped in awe as he stared at a lightly discolored, but healed, line where the cut had been in his skin.

Back in Judea, the marketplace bustled. The streets were crowded, making it perfect for a person of certain fame to go unnoticed. Not that Roman soldiers ever escaped unnoticed in a Jewish village.

Ever since Tyquavius witnessed an empty tomb three days after the Nazorean's crucifixion, he was reassigned to market duty in the attempt to help him forget that day. At the moment he stood leaned against a fruit stand, arms crossed. He'd had a bit too much to drink the night before, so he found himself closing his eyes now and then.

Suddenly there was a whisper in his ear, "Can you tell me where I can buy a slab of pork?"

His eyes, bloodshot, opened instantly. "Look, I don't care if you defile your own religion by not eating kosher, but—" Tyquavius turned to face the person speaking.

Clad in old ragged clothes that Aron had let him borrow, Cassius stared at his friend with a sly smirk.

"Cass? Cass, you can't be here!" Tyquavius ushered Cassius with an arm under the elbow and steered him away from the market crowd.

In a narrow alley, Tyquavius checked in all directions to make sure they were alone. "There's an order to have you arrested and exiled, stripped of your rank."

"An order from Pilate?"

Tyquavius shook his head. "Aurelius."

"I'm not surprised."

"Why are you here?"

Cassius' smile hardened. "I need to know what happened at the Nazorean's tomb."

Tyquavius was fully sober now. "Nothing. It was just a hallucination. I didn't drink enough water that day."

"That's what they want you to believe. Have you forgotten that I was there when Caiaphas paid you to keep silent?"

Leaning against the side of a linen shop, Tyquavius began panting and shuddering. He brought his hands to his face and muttered as if he'd gone mad.

"What's wrong with you?" Cassius took his friend by the shoulders and shook lightly.

Tyquavius met Cassius' eyes, and Cassius nearly froze with fear at this sudden seriousness.

"That man I watched get crucified—I saw him walk out of his grave like he had just woken up from a nap. I can't stop replaying the scene in my mind, but I have to put on a brave face. It's the Roman way. It's who we are. I can't afford to get all wobbly and emotional over something I still don't truly understand."

Tyquavius, as he confessed, slid down the wall. Instead of standing, he had crumbled to the ground, nearly in a fetal position. Cassius knelt down to comfort him as best he could.

"Ty, I believe I do understand." He dug around in the satchel he had draped over his shoulder and showed an end of the Nazorean's garment to Tyquavius. "The lot. This garment. I can't quite explain it, but it heals people and animals. It worked on me and performed a miracle on Livy."

Just then, a voice echoed around the corner. "Tyquavius, your post!" Crunchy footsteps grew louder and Marcus appeared. At the site of the friends on the ground, one being a wanted man, Marcus paused and gaped.

But Marcus had a duty. "Someone go and summon Aurelius!" he shouted. "Cassius has returned!"

Tyquavius shot upright. "Cass, go before they find you."

Cassius shook his head. "I'm not afraid of Aurelius."

"You should be."

"No, he should be afraid of me. I know where I have to go, and he can follow me if wants me bad enough."

On his horse, Cassius tore off out of the city. However, it wasn't long until he had company storming behind him. Although he couldn't distinguish every soldier who was behind him, he knew that Aurelius was leading the calvary.

When Cassius arrived at Jesus' tomb, he cursed himself for forgetting that Pilate and the high priests had the entrance double blocked. Besides the cork-shaped boulder that typically sealed tombs, several other bulky boulders stood in the way. He jumped from the horse and tied the bloodstained garment around his waist for safekeeping.

Aurelius and his mob came on scene shortly thereafter. He let out a long, bellowing laugh. "Where do you think you're going to hide, boy, inside a tomb?"

Truth be told, Cassius didn't actually know what he had planned. He knew that the garment and its miraculous powers might save him in a bind if Aurelius were to have swords drawn on him. Otherwise, the tomb was just an isolated fortress.

The laughing faded as Cassius attempted to move a boulder.

Aurelius said, "My poor Livy is smitten. She stays in her room and sobs over your sorry bones. She's in love with a traitor, and that's unacceptable."

"I saved her," Cassius answered, "no thanks to you."

"Curb your tongue, traitor!" Aurelius snipped. "Remember that I gave you everything you needed to become a proud soldier of this country. I treated you like a son and provided you with all the best training and resources. And how do you repay me? A brazen love affair with my own daughter! I will have you flogged and exiled for such a disgrace."

Cassius straightened himself and looked Aurelius dead in the eye. "Try your luck. I'm not alone."

Just then Cassius heard the same voice he had heard that day at the well.

"*Sequi...Sequi...*"

As he turned back towards the empty tomb and heard the jostling of horses preparing to charge after him, the ground began to quake. It was a gentle shaking at first, but it soon grew into an unsteady rumbling.

Cassius clutched jagged boulders as he staggered his way to the tomb entrance. He dared to turn around when he heard shouting behind him.

Aurelius had lost control of his horse's reins and in turn plummeted to the ground. Meanwhile Cornelius and Marcus were trying to steady their horses and turn back towards the city. The other soldiers stumbled in the chaos.

Finally Cassius managed his way to the entrance and worked on pushing back the main rock that guarded the tomb. The wind started to pick up as he groaned and pushed even harder. Specks of dust and dirt stung his face. The ground still shook, but it was clear that now a dust storm was to follow this earthquake.

His arms were weak and sore, but he was almost there. With one last surge of adrenaline, he moved the stone back enough so he could slip inside the tomb and wait out these freak natural disasters.

Were they actually freak incidents?

In amazement, he examined the interior of the tomb, gently passing his fingertips over the cold stone slab where a body once lay. But not just any body. He untied the garment from his waist and carefully draped it over the slab. This garment did not belong to him. It was never his to keep. Not for a Roman soldier who barely knew what powers a monotheistic god could wield.

He sat on the floor of the tomb and leaned his back against the wall. He brought his knees to his chin as if he were a boy. This was his time to rest. He closed his eyes, but visions of Livy's beautiful and ageless face danced in his mind. Sometimes he wished he'd never bet on that lot, but then Livy would've likely died from blood loss.

Looking around the hollow tomb, Cassius couldn't help but wonder what had really happened in this space. Had the long-awaited

Jewish messiah truly risen from the dead here? The garment was far from the ivory color it had been, and there were frays at the seams. He didn't know much about what it meant to be holy, as he came from a Roman culture of multiple angry gods who care little for humans. But as he continued to sit in this hallowed space, he was curious. He was anxious. He knew he couldn't go back to his old life. It was time for something new and inspiring.

The earth grew still again and the wind died down. He heard a voice, almost a whisper that he couldn't distinguish. Then he got to his feet, folded the garment, tucked it under his arm, and followed the voice to the tomb entrance. He threw a hand above his eyes to block the sun. Aurelius and the soldiers had gone. All that remained was Cassius, a horse, and a bloodied garment.

"Sequi...Sequi...Sequi..."

Cassius mounted his horse and headed in the direction of the tender voice. Perhaps he had won the lot after all.

About the Author

Nicole Fratrich is an author, blogger, poet, teacher, and active Catholic with a bachelor's degree in English from Saint Vincent College. She has been published in *Mystery Weekly*, *Twofer Compendium*, and the *Loyalhanna Review*. In 2024, she was voted the 4th best author in the Johnstown, Pennsylvania area. Check out her other books: *The Music Makes the Man* (historical fiction) and *Rowdy's Popcorn Adventure* (children's book). Read her whole bio at www.nicolefratrichauthor.com and peruse her blog, Confessions of a Classic Soul (www.coacs.home.blog).